Christmas Wombat

by Jackie French

illustrated by

Bruce Whatley

Clarion Books • Houghton Mifflin Harcourt • Boston / New York • 2012

To Beth, with love and wombats
J.F.

For Lana, Lincoln, and Harry—Merry Christmas
B.W.

Clarion Books
215 Park Avenue South,
New York, New York 10003

First published in Australia in 2011 by Angus & Robertson,
an imprint of HarperCollins Publishers, Australia.
Published in the United States in 2012.

Clarion Books is an imprint of Houghton Mifflin Harcourt Publishing Company.

www.hmhbooks.com

The illustrations were executed in acrylic paints on watercolor paper.
The text was set in Kid's Stuff Plain.

Library of Congress Cataloging-in-Publication Data is available.
ISBN 978-0-547-86872-1

Manufactured in China

10 9 8 7 6 5 4 3 2 1

4500339555

I'm a wombat.

I live in Australia.

My home is a hole in the ground.

I enjoy sleeping, scratching, and eating.

Especially eating.

Especially eating carrots.

Slept.

Scratched.

Slept.

Ate grass.

Dangly things bumped against my nose.

Got rid of them.

Smelled carrots!

Strange creatures are eating my carrots!

Fought major battle
with strange creatures.

Won the battle.

Feeling tired.

Found the perfect spot
to have a nap.

zzzzzzzzzZ

I smell **carrots**!

Strange creatures trying
to eat my carrots!

Got rid of them.
Again.

Carrots delicious.

Off to find MORE carrots.

A wombat hole?

Carrots!

Needed help
getting back up.

Scratched.

Have misjudged
strange creatures.
They can be useful
for finding carrots.

Never knew there were so many carrots in the world!

Carrots . . .

Carrots . . .

My
Carrots!

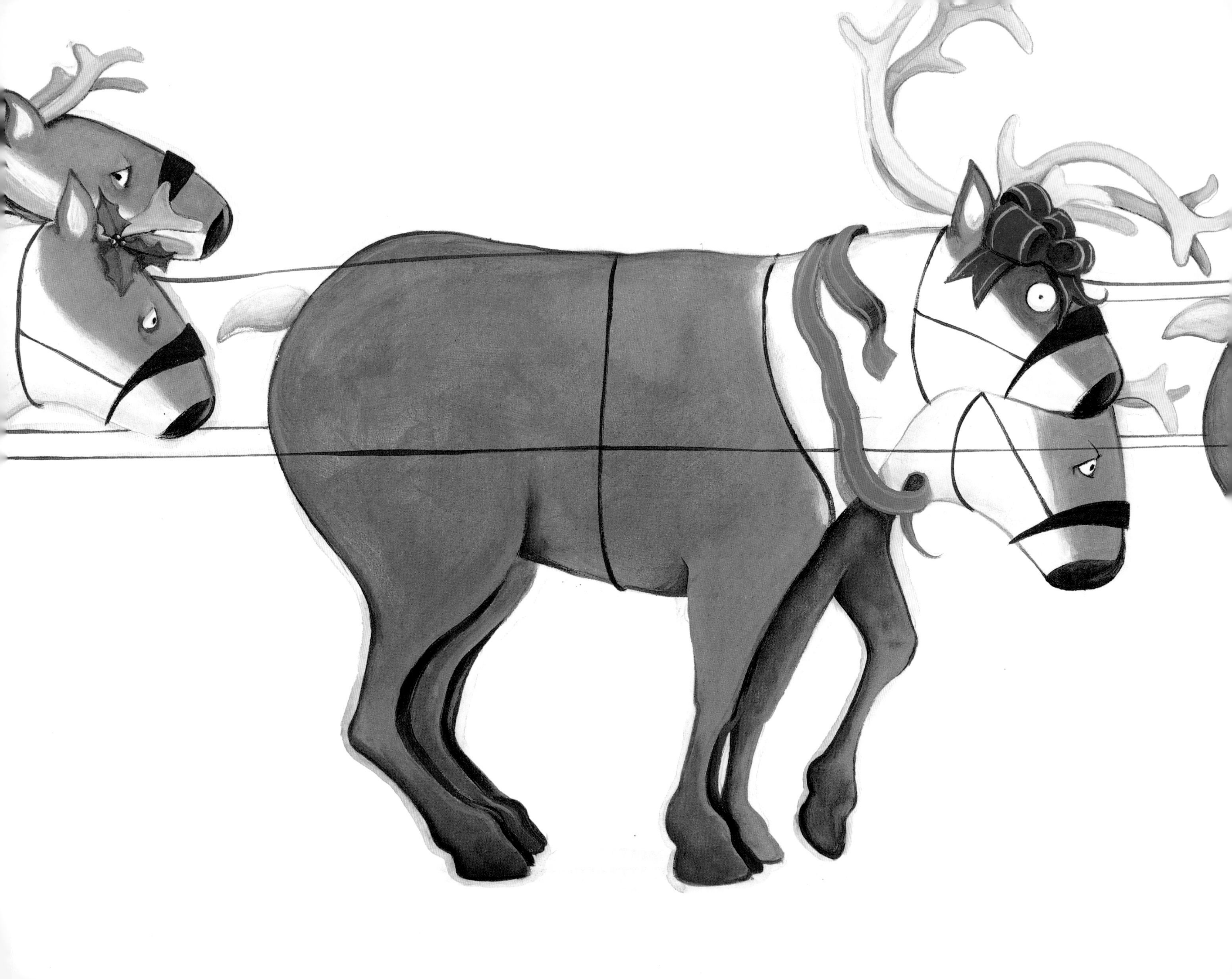

Said goodbye to
strange creatures.
Hope they visit
again soon.

Grass delicious . . . but for some reason not hungry.

Slept.